THE THREE BILLY

JERRY

A long time ago, on the rocky side of a river, there lived a family of three hungry billy goats Gruff. The wild grasses flourished on the other side of the river, where the sun always shone brightest. And under the bridge passing over that water, there lived a troll with a heart of stone, who guarded the crossing day and night.

The billy goats became so tempted by the tasty-looking grasses that they were determined to get to the other side of the river. But the water was deep and full of fish—some of them even larger than the goats. The littlest and hungriest goat was the first to march toward the crossing.

Trip, trap! Trip, trap!

Bravely, that little billy goat Gruff trotted across the bridge.

Trip, trap! Trip, trap!

Trip, trap!

"WHO'S THAT TRIP-TRAPPING
OVER MY BRIDGE?"
roared the selfish troll.

Trip, trap!
Trip, trap!

"It's only I," the littlest billy goat squeaked.
"I'm heading up the hillside to make myself fat."

"I'm going to gobble you up!"
declared the troll.

"Oh, no, don't eat me!" cried the littlest goat.
"Wait until the next billy goat crosses.
He's much bigger than me."

"Well, go on then! You're nothing but skin and bones, and I want to fix a hearty stew!"

munch, munch

Next, the second billy goat Gruff stomped across the bridge.

Trip, trap!

Trip, trap!

"WHO'S THAT TRIP-TRAPPING OVER MY BRIDGE?"
shouted the nasty troll.

"It's only I," the second billy goat bleated.
"I'm heading up the hillside to make myself fat!"

"I'm going to gobble you up!"
the troll growled.

"Oh, no, don't eat me," begged the second goat.
"Big Billy Goat Gruff will be crossing soon."

"Then get out of the way,
you scrawny creature!

Big Billy Goat will make a much tastier meal!"

munch,
munch

Before long, the biggest billy goat Gruff
stormed across the bridge.

"**It is I,**" the biggest billy goat announced.
"I'm heading up the hillside to make myself fat."

"WHO'S THAT TRIP-TRAPPING OVER MY BRIDGE?"

howled the greedy troll.

The troll scowled.

The goat charged.

Then, *BAM!*

Trip, trap! Trip, trap!

But the troll was probably a bit too sour and green to make a tasty meal.

The troll watched in defeat as a herd of billy goats joined their friends on the hillside.

And over where the sun shone brightest and the wild grasses flourished, the billy goats would fill their bellies.

ARTIST'S NOTE

I have wanted to retell "The Three Billy Goats Gruff" for as long as I have been making books that reimagine classic tales. Over the years, countless teachers, librarians, and storytellers have declared it a favorite classroom read-aloud, and I was deeply drawn to the drama of the story: It demands heightened animation in the telling, with multiple voices and an arc of tension that builds to a crescendo, inviting plenty of audience participation. I was, however, confounded by the ending of the original tale, in which the troll disappears or turns to stone when tossed into the water; it seemed he never had a chance to learn his lesson.

I invented the character of the giant fish to offer a way for the troll to recognize what he'd done to others and to experience his word-bullying from another point of view. I also longed for the story to be more than a cautionary tale or a revenge story where the victim resorts to violence. In this version, readers can still cheer for the underdogs—even when the troll gets his due—but careful observers of the endpaper art may be left with the sense that there could be a turning point in this relationship. It's up to the reader to ask questions and finish the story: Has the troll learned his lesson? Does he redeem himself? Is forgiveness an option for the goats? Can these characters ever have a peaceful coexistence? These are important questions not just in children's everyday lives, but in the world at large.

Artistically, the story was an intriguing challenge because it is so compact: It all takes place on one small bridge, and yet there are four equally important characters, each page with a big emotional moment. Attending to size relationships, creating distinct personalities for the goats, and evoking strong human emotions from animals that needed to remain mostly naturalistic were all details that required focus. Photo reference is limited for these amazing animals often regarded primarily as petting-zoo inhabitants, so I used miniature models of goats to help create fresh perspectives. Ultimately it was only my imagination, however, that could invent the characters of these ever-so-relatable billy goats Gruff. They are, like many of us, both meek and at the same time strong in the face of adversity… and they must work together to "stand up to the bullies" and be a force for change.

To all of my fellow Capricorns. —

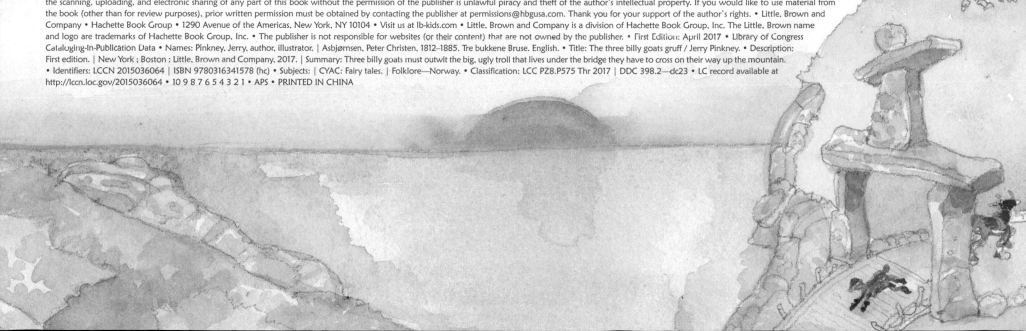

The art for this book was created using pencil and watercolor on Arches cold-pressed paper. This book was edited by Andrea Spooner and designed by Saho Fujii. The production was supervised by Erika Schwartz, and the production editor was Jen Graham. This book was printed on 140gsm Gold Sun wood-free paper. The text was set in Maiandra, and the display type was hand-lettered.